For Paulette — who always makes sure I stay on the path.

For information about permission to reproduce selections from this book,
please contact permissions@astrapublishinghouse.com.

mineditionUS
An imprint of Astra Books for Young Readers, a division of Astra Publishing House
astrapublishinghouse.com
This book was printed in October 2021 at Grafiche AZ, Verona (BA), Italy.

ISBN 978-1-6626-5063-5
eISBN: 978-1-6626-5078-9
Library of Congress Cataloging-in-Publication Data available upon request.

First Impression

10 9 8 7 6 5 4 3 2 1

This book was illustrated digitally and typeset in New Baskerville.
It was edited by Maria Russo and Leonard Marcus, and designed by
Bob Staake and Micheal Neuegebauer.

The Path

Bob Staake

minedition

You will walk.

You will walk along a well-worn path
that many others have taken before you.

Often the path will be easy.
Flat, and simple.

It may take you over gentle.
grassy hills shaded by towering
trees that sway in the breeze.

The path might weave
through valleys of
wildflowers bathed in
the warm sunlight.

But sometimes it will become bumpy and difficult. It may even be blocked by obstacles that you will need to overcome.

It may meander through dark,
scary forests shadowed in mystery
and easy to become lost in.

The path will zig and zag up
steep and challenging hills that
appear impossible to climb.

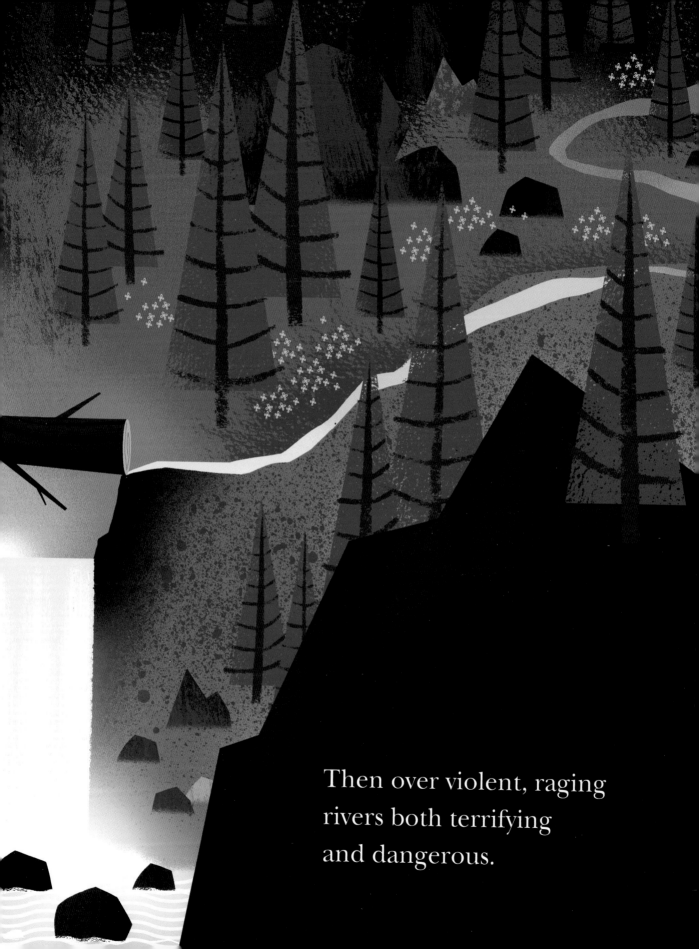

Then over violent, raging
rivers both terrifying
and dangerous.

When the path becomes muddy
alongside a pond or through a
soggy swamp, walking may be
hard and your journey may slow.

And when it leads into a sunless,
chilly cave it may seem as if the
path will simply end.

It won't.

The path will surprise you . . .

. . . as it splits into two different directions.

How will you know which way to go?

You will know.

You will know because those two choices
are not the only possibilities.

You will know because like all the others
who have walked the path before you . . .

. . . you too will create
your *own* path.